The Speech of Love

A Sweet Small Town Medical Romance

Amber Rose Clifford

Contents

Chapter 1

Emily

The door swings open and there's Lily, her little hand clutching her momma's. Her big brown eyes find mine and she gives me a shy smile.

"Well hey there, sweet pea!" I say, bending down to her level. "Are you ready for some fun today?"

Lily nods, still not saying anything. Her momma strokes her hair, and she leans into her hand.

"We've been practicing those exercises you gave us," her momma says. "She's getting better every day."

"That's wonderful! Great job, Lily!" I say. I lead them over to the little table where we do our sessions. Lily plops down in her special chair, the one with a large sunflower painted on the back.

I pull out the box of toys and games I use for speech therapy—puzzles, picture books, flash cards. While Lily digs through, I ask her momma the usual questions about how their week has been. Inside, I'm itching to get started. I just love helping this little girl find her voice.

"Okay, Lily, let's warm up with a game," I say, holding up two hand puppets. "Want to help me tell a story?"

Lily grins and takes the puppets, moving their mouths silently as I narrate a silly tale about two friends going on adventures. I pause often, encouraging Lily to fill in words or repeat phrases after me.

When she stumbles over a sound, I wait patiently, my voice gentle. "That's okay, take your time, Lily. You've got this."

Lily beams every time she conquers a tricky word. My heart swells looking at that smile. This is why I do what I do.

The session flies by. Before I know it, Lily's momma is glancing at her watch.

"Time sure does fly when we're having fun!" I say. I turn to Lily. "You did so great today, Lily. I'm so proud of you!"

Lily's little face lights up. She hops down and goes to take her momma's hand.

"Thank you, Emily," her momma says. "We've seen such improvement since starting here."

I wave as they head out the door into the late afternoon sunlight. Another good day. Another child finding their voice. This is what it's all about.

The sun is dipping low as I make my way to Hazel's Cafe to meet my best friend, Sarah, for our weekly catch-up. I smile, picturing her sitting in our usual corner booth, two steaming mugs waiting on the table.

I push open the door, breathing in the scent of fresh pie and coffee. The dinner crowd chatters around me, familiar faces smiling in greeting.

"Emily, great to see you!" My friend, Max, owner of this bustling establishment, calls out from behind the counter, waving me over. "The usual for you and Sarah?"

"You know it," I say with a grin. "Though I hope you have a slice of pecan waiting for us, too."

Max laughs. "Come on now, have I ever forgotten your favorite?"

I wink and head to the back. There's Sarah, her auburn hair falling across her cheek as she scans the specials board, her freckles seeming to dance over her face under the twinkling lights.

She turns as I slide in across from her. "Emily! I feel like I haven't seen you in ages. So much has happened in the last week."

We fall into easy conversation about our weeks. I tell her about Lily's progress and my new client intake. She vents about parent-teacher conferences, but her eyes shine sharing a story about her students putting on a play.

Soon we're gossiping and giggling like schoolgirls over town rumors. It hasn't been long since I last saw her, but I realize I've missed this, missed my best friend. When I'm not with her, it's like all I do is focus on work. Any spare moment goes to tending to my beloved garden.

A lull falls. Sarah regards me closely. "So...any men on the horizon for you? Or are you married to your job, as always?"

I snort. "You know me, all work and no play." But her words give me pause. It has been a while since I've let someone in.

"Well, you can't live in that clinic forever," Sarah teases.

I just smile softly. Maybe she's right. Maybe it's time to open my heart again.

But it's a small town, and I know pretty much everybody. It seems like the good men around here are all married or taken, or have moved away to live a faster-paced life. Anyway, men just sound like an unnecessary distraction. There are so many children I can help to find their voices again. To take myself away from that for a moment of fun and excitement just seems selfish.

I give Sarah a warm hug goodbye and head out into the cool evening air. The sun is just starting to set, casting a warm glow over the quiet streets of our little town.

I take my time walking home, enjoying the peace of this place I've always called home. I pass the library, the corner market, the church. Everyone is settling in for the night.

Soon I'm turning down the tree-lined lane leading to my cozy cottage. I stop to admire my garden, the flowers nodding their heads for the night.

Inside, I put on some tea and start prepping a simple salad and baked chicken for dinner. I find myself humming as I work. Despite Sarah's teasing, I really do enjoy my solitary evenings like this.

After eating, I tidy up and then head back outside with my gardening gloves and tools. I kneel down to inspect the rose bushes I've been carefully cultivating.

"Well aren't you beauties coming in nicely," I murmur. I prune and shape with care, losing myself in the work. Twilight gardening really is one of my favorite things.

Before long, the light fades completely. I stand, brushing dirt from my knees, and take one last deep breath of the fresh night air before going back inside.

I change into comfy pajamas and then curl up on the sofa with my latest novel, a thriller by a local author who I went to school with. The mystery immediately pulls me in. I'll have to let her know I'm really enjoying this one next time I see her at the local bookstore.

Curled up with my book and a cup of chamomile tea, listening to the gentle sounds of night settling around my little cottage, I feel a deep sense of contentment. This is my happy place.

My mind drifts back to my conversation with Sarah. Maybe someday I'll make room in my life for someone to share this with. But for now, I have everything I need right here.

I read a few more chapters before switching off the lamp and heading to my bedroom, perfectly at peace. Ichange into my comfy pajamas, settle into bed, and pick up my journal from the nightstand. I always take a few minutes before sleep to reflect on my day.

I write about my session with Lily and how proud I felt seeing her gain confidence with each exercise. Her stutter has improved so much in just a few short weeks. I know how frustrating it can be for kids when they struggle to communicate, and it literally affects almost every facet of their lives—their behavior, their success at school, their relationship with other children and adults. Helping Lily find her voice is so rewarding.

My work is not always easy, but moments like today make it all worthwhile. Seeing that spark of joy in Lily's eyes when she succeeded in an activity she found difficult before gives me a profound sense of purpose.

I'm thankful I get to do what I love in this little town I call home. My cozy house, loyal friends, and meaningful work - what more could I need? This simple life suits me perfectly.

I close my journal, turn off the light, and snuggle into my covers. As I drift off, I whisper a silent prayer of thanks for another fulfilling day. The last image in my mind is Lily's proud smile. My heart is full.

Chapter 2

♥

Ryan

The morning sun glints off my windshield as I cruise down Main Street. White picket fences and flower boxes line the sidewalks. An old man in dark blue overalls waters his lawn while a pair of kids chase each other around a magnolia tree. This Norman Rockwell painting of a town is worlds away from the frenetic energy of the city I left behind.

I pull up to a quaint little diner called "Maggie's" and step inside. The bell above the door jingles merrily.

"Mornin'!" calls the waitress as she wipes down the counter. "Haven't seen you before, hon. You just passin' through?"

"Yes ma'am," I reply. "Name's Ryan. Just rolled into town this morning."

"Well hey there, Ryan. I'm Maggie. Welcome to Sweetwater!" She smiles warmly. "Coffee while you look over the menu?"

"That'd be great, thanks."

I take a seat at the counter as Maggie pours me a steaming cup. The aroma is downright heavenly.

Two men in plaid shirts sit nearby, talking crops and weather. An elderly couple shares a slice of some kind of mouthwatering pie. A family with a gaggle of kids takes up the corner booth. Everyone seems to know each other.

As Maggie takes my order, she chats about her grandkids and asks if I have family in town. I find myself opening up, telling her I'm a doctor starting work at the local clinic.

"Well, bless your heart! Aren't we lucky to have you."

Her kindness catches me off guard. I can't remember the last time a stranger took such an interest in my life back in the city. It felt more robotic there, full of self-interest and climbing the rungs of what corporate ladder you found yourself on.

As I sip my coffee and watch the locals banter, a feeling washes over me that I haven't felt in years - a sense of belonging. It's hard to explain, seeing I just got here, but I immediately feel very welcome. I was resistant to the idea at first, moving to a place like this. But this friendly little town may be just what I need. A fresh start.

I finish up my meal at the diner, lingering a bit to soak up the cozy small-town vibe. But I can't sit here all afternoon - I've got to get settled into my new place.

The apartment the clinic set me up with is just a few blocks off Main Street. It's a modest one-bedroom, simply furnished but with all the necessities. The walls are bare, save for a generic landscape painting left by the previous tenant.

I set my suitcase on the bed and take stock of my sparse surroundings. This sterile apartment is a far cry from my sleek high-rise back in the city with all its smart appliances and other conveniences I took for granted or barely used. But I try to see it as a blank canvas, a chance to start fresh. A simpler life.

After unpacking the essentials, I pull out my phone to call Alex. My cousin and I went through undergrad together, but our careers sent us on different paths. He's now a top corporate attorney at a prestigious downtown law firm.

Alex picks up on the second ring. "Ryan! You make it to the sticks alright?"

I laugh. "If by 'sticks' you mean the idyllic small town of Sweetwater, then yes. The drive was beautiful, Alex. Rolling green hills, farms, a cute little Main Street lined with mom and pop shops. It's crazy different from the concrete jungle we're used to."

Alex chuckles. "I'll take your word for it, man. But as long as they have a clinic that needs a talented doctor, that's all that matters, right?"

"Of course," I reply. "This residency is an important step. I know I need to focus on becoming the best physician I can be."

But privately, I wonder if there's more in store for me in this quaint town. A chance to connect with people on a deeper level. To learn what really matters, far from the frenetic hard-heartedness of the city. It could be just what I need to become not only a better doctor, but a better person.

The next morning I make my way to the clinic for my first day. Like most things in this town, it's located in a small brick building on Main Street, nestled between a pharmacy and a flower shop. As I walk up to the entrance, I notice locals already lined up waiting for the doors to open.

I'm greeted by a friendly older nurse named Janet. "You must be Dr. Mitchell! We're so happy to have you. Let me give you a quick tour before we open up."

Janet shows me around the cozy clinic which is clean and well-maintained. Despite its modest size, it seems well equipped, even featuring some medical equipment I didn't expect to see here. More importantly, the staff have an easy camaraderie that speaks to the close-knit community.

We run into Dr. Simmons, the clinic director. "Welcome, Dr. Mitchell! We may not be the biggest clinic, but our patients are like family here. You'll get to know them all quite well. They were very excited to hear a new doctor was going to be joining us for a while. They're ready to see a new face instead of mine," he laughs.

I smile, taking in the personal touches everywhere like the artwork created by local schoolchildren that is proudly displayed all over the walls. "I can already sense the care you have for your patients, Dr. Simmons. It's refreshing and inspiring."

As patients start trickling in, I shadow Janet, observing the thoughtful attention she gives each person. She asks about family members, remembers personal details. No rushed visits here. No quotas to get through to avoid cutthroat businesspeople breathing down your neck.

This is exactly the change I needed. I can feel it in my bones already—this town, this clinic, these people have something special to teach me. I'm right where I need to be.

Chapter 3

Emily

I hurry through the clinic doors, the familiar hustle and bustle enveloping me like a warm hug. Little Connor has come so far in his speech therapy - I can't wait to see how he does with those tricky R sounds today.

My thoughts are interrupted when I collide with a tall figure in the hallway, sending a cascade of files flying. "Oh my gosh, I'm so sorry!" I exclaim, immediately kneeling to gather the papers. I may be good at helping give children their voice back, but I really need to work on my clumsiness.

"No harm done," the man says with an easy smile. He's the new doctor, I realize as I notice his doctor's coat and stethoscope. And cute, some unprofessional part of my brain registers.

We stand awkwardly over the haphazard pile of files between us. "I'm Emily, the speech therapist here," I offer.

"Ryan. The new doctor," he says, motioning at his stethoscope. "It's a pleasure to meet you."

I feel myself blush, despite my best efforts to remain professional. "Likewise. I apologize again for the collision. I don't make a habit of crashing into new doctors in hallways."

"Think nothing of it." Ryan's eyes crinkle warmly. "I looked over today's files and hear you've been doing great work with young Connor. It takes a special kind of dedication to connect with kids like that."

Now I'm really blushing. "Aw, thanks. Connor's a real sweetheart. We've just been taking it one step at a time."

Ryan nods. "Well, keep up the good work. I look forward to working with you."

We exchange a lingering glance before I give a little wave and continue down the hall, heart fluttering. Lawd have mercy. The new doctor's got me all aflutter. But I'd best keep my wits about me. Wouldn't wanna let some handsome man sweep me off my feet...or would I?

I take a deep breath as I push open the door to Max's cafe, the little bell above the door announcing my arrival with a cheerful jingle. The rich aroma of freshly brewed coffee envelops me like a warm hug.

"There's my girl!" Max calls out from behind the counter, his freckled face breaking into a wide smile. "The usual?"

"You know it," I say, settling onto my favorite stool at the counter. Max slides a steaming mug of coffee in front of me, topped with a perfect swirl of whipped cream and a sprinkle of demerara sugar.

"So what's new in the world of Emily today?" he asks, leaning forward conspiratorially.

I take a sip, savoring the bold flavor. "Oh, not much. Just had a run-in with the new doctor over at the clinic." I blush. "A literal run-in. I ran into him in the hallway."

Max raises an eyebrow. "The young handsome one all the nurses are fussin' over?"

I roll my eyes, but can't help grinning. "I mean, he is rather dashing. But I barely know the man, Max! And I think he just got into town. Those nurses don't waste any time!"

"Mmhmm, sure," Max says with a wink. "Nothin' wrong with appreciatin' a fine figure of a man."

"Max!" I exclaim, swatting his arm playfully. "You know my policy - no dating colleagues. Especially ones who are just here temporarily."

Max shakes his head. "You and your rules, Emily. Ain't no harm in being open to new possibilities." His expression softens. "I know you've been hurt before, honey. But don't let fear close your heart entirely."

I stare down into my coffee, pensive. Max is right, as usual. Since my last relationship ended badly, I've been wary to open myself to romance again. But maybe...just maybe...this Ryan could be different. I'm getting ahead of myself, though. I just met the man. And even though he's cute, for all I know he could be a right jerk. He might not even be a very good doctor.

"I'll think on it," I say finally. "Just gonna take things real slow."

Max smiles warmly. "There's my wise girl. Trust your heart, Emily. It won't lead you astray."

I nod slowly, turning over Max's advice in my mind. He always seems to know just what to say.

After I finish my coffee, I give Max a quick hug and head out into the sunny afternoon. I decide to stop by the library to return some books before my next appointment.

As I walk in, I immediately spot an unfamiliar figure browsing the shelves - it's Dr. Ryan! Before I can duck out of sight, he glances up and notices me.

"Emily! Fancy seeing you here," he says with a friendly smile. He's even more handsome up close, with warm brown eyes and a strong jawline.

"Dr. Ryan, hello again," I reply, hoping I'm not blushing. "I see you've already found our local library."

"Please, call me Ryan when we're not at the clinic," he insists. "I had some free time and was just familiarizing myself with the town's history. It's fascinating how interconnected everyone here seems to be."

I relax a bit, leaning against the shelf. "Yes, we're a close-knit community. I've lived here my whole life, so I can barely remember when I didn't know everyone."

Ryan nods thoughtfully. "The librarian, Lily, was telling me all about the various families and local legends. She seems to know everything about this place."

"Oh, Lily's a character for sure," I chuckle. "She loves sharing stories about our quirky little town."

Ryan smiles. "Well, it certainly seems like an interesting place. And the people here are so warm and welcoming. Especially you, Emily."

I feel my cheeks flush again under his earnest gaze. Get it together, girl! I scold myself.

"I, um, should get going," I stammer. "But let me know if you ever want to hear more about our unique little community."

"I'd like that," Ryan says sincerely.

I offer him a parting smile, then slip away, my heart beating just a little faster. Maybe I won't rule out getting to know this new doctor after all. There's just something about him that makes me think the risk could be worth it.

Chapter 4

Emily

I look up from the file cabinet as the clinic door opens, the little bell above it tinkling merrily. Ryan walks in, right on time as usual, his button-down shirt neatly pressed, his doctor's coat strewn over his muscular forearm.

"Mornin' Emily," he says, flashing me that charming crooked smile of his.

"Hey there, Dr. Ryan," I say, unable to keep from grinning back. I love that he called me by my first name. There's a familiarity to it that makes me feel like we're more than just colleagues.

We get to work seeing patients, falling into an easy rhythm. I handle the therapies while he provides the medical oversight. Like dance partners, we complement each other perfectly.

Around mid-morning, Old Mrs. Jenkins shuffles in. She's been coming to see me for years, ever since her stroke. It takes her a while to get her words out, but we have ourselves a nice visit every week. Often, I think it's more about the company for her than anything else, and I'm not in a rush so I'm happy to provide companionship when I can. I give her a hug and notice a new drawing from one of her grandkids on the thank you wall behind us.

"Aren't they precious?" I say to Ryan as Mrs. Jenkins makes her slow way out.

He gazes at the wall covered in childish scribbles and smiles. "This place really is the heart of the community, isn't it?"

"Sure is," I reply, feeling that familiar swell of pride. "Our patients are just like family here. My own artwork used to be proudly displayed up there, too," I laugh.

Ryan's still staring at the wall, looking thoughtful. I wonder if maybe this small town doc is starting to feel at home here after all.

The Next Day

The sun shines birghtly through the windows of the community center as I set up for our big spring carnival. This is one of my favorite events of the year. The whole town turns out for games, crafts, music - just good old-fashioned fun.

I'm in charge of the children's booth, so I'm covering the tables with bright paper and getting out bins of crayons, paints and other art supplies. Across the room, Sarah is organizing the bake sale table, which is already overflowing with pies, cookies and cakes made by the local ladies. The smells are heavenly.

"Hey Emily, where do you want these puppets for the puppet show?" asks Max, lugging in a big box.

"Oh, just set them on the stage for now," I tell him. Max has been helping coordinate the carnival entertainment, a rare break from his seemingly endless shifts at the cafe.

I look around at all the colorful banners and artwork decorating the community center. This place is the heart and soul of our little town.

Just then a minor crisis erupts. Two volunteers get into a heated debate over the dunk tank location. Before things escalate too far, I quickly step in to mediate. It's not the first disagreement I've smoothed over around here. "Bob, it'll be great. I promise you'll both get dunked!"

Max chuckles as the two walk away muttering apologies. "You're not just our speech therapist, you know. You're like the ambassador for this whole dang town!"

I laugh and continue hanging up some of the children's art projects from my clinic. "Well, someone's gotta make sure our traditions and values stay strong around here."

Yep, it's a busy day, but there's nowhere I'd rather be. This is what community is all about.

I take a deep breath of the fresh summer air as I step into the town square, which has been transformed for the lively festival. The cobblestone streets are lined with local artisans selling their wares - handmade quilts, wood carvings, jars of homemade jams. My mouth waters as I pass the pie stall, inhaling the sweet aroma of apple and cherry.

I wave to familiar faces all around me. Little Lily runs up to show me the woven bracelet she made at the craft booth. "It's beautiful!" I tell her, admiring her work. She beams with pride before scampering off to play ring toss.

In the distance, I hear the upbeat sound of fiddles and banjos. People are two-stepping near the bandstand, keeping rhythm with the fast-paced music. I sway along as I make my way through the crowd, exchanging warm greetings and hugs.

Out of the corner of my eye, I notice Ryan meandering aimlessly through the festivities. He seems a bit overwhelmed, but also curious, taking in all the sights and sounds. I can't relate to that, having lived here all my life. I've never felt like an outsider in Sweetwater. But I've seen the community welcome newcomers with open arms, and I'll sure they'll be more than happy to do the same for a handsome young doctor.

As I continue mingling, I keep an eye on Ryan. When he wanders near the bandstand, I catch his gaze and motion for him to join me under the string lights off to the side, away from the commotion.

"So, what do you think of our little festival?" I ask.

Ryan smiles. "I've never experienced anything like this before. The energy, the people...it's incredible."

He pauses, looking thoughtful. "Back in the city, I didn't even know my neighbor's name. But here, you all support each other like family."

I nod. "That's small town living for you. We may not have glitzy malls or nightlife, but we have heart and tradition. This place has a way of growing on you."

Ryan meets my eyes. "I wasn't sure what to expect, but I think I'm starting to understand that now," he says with a grin.

Chapter 5

Ryan

I sit at my rickety dining table, clutching a chipped mug of coffee as I stare out the window. Beyond the peeling paint and stained carpet of my modest apartment, the sleepy streets of this small town stretch out before me. Gone are the glaring lights and honking horns of the big city - instead, a peaceful quiet blankets the neighborhood as the day winds down.

I take a sip of weak, tepid coffee and sigh. My mind wanders back to the relentless pace of life in the city, the ruthless corporate ladder I'd been climbing. I'd lived and breathed work, chasing the next promotion, the next raise. Packing my schedule with grueling workout routines and time-consuming dates with vapid women who pushed very expensive lettuce leaves around their plates while lamenting the latest reality TV show fight. I barely had time for anything else.

But now...things are different. Here in this sleepy town, I've found a sense of community. Like yesterday, when old Mrs. Johnson's sink sprung a leak. Half the neighborhood showed up to help fix it. Then we all sat on her creaky porch drinking sweet tea and swapping stories until sunset.

I smile faintly at the memory. Back in the city, you'd be lucky if your neighbor nodded your way in the elevator. But here...people care about each other. My ambitions don't seem as important as they once did. The me of a few weeks ago would laugh at the me of today.

"What is it I really want?" I murmur, staring down into my coffee. The simple life I'm building here is so fulfilling. But my drive to succeed, to climb to the top...that hunger still burns inside me. And this is only meant to be temporary anyway. A rotation. The fact I'm even contemplating what it would be like to stay here longer, to make things more permanent, is a little baffling to me.

I'm torn between two worlds. With a sigh, I take another sip of tepid coffee. All I know is that I've only been in this little town for a short time, but it has already changed the way I see the world. And I have some hard thinking to do about what future I want to build.

Emily

The walls of my clinic envelop me in a soothing blanket of familiarity as I prepare for my next appointment. In my office, hand-painted murals of birds and flowers cover the walls, bringing the calming hues of nature indoors. A bookshelf overflowing with dog-eared children's books, tubs of art supplies, and bins of textured toys provide tools for connecting with my young patients.

A knock at the door pulls me from my thoughts. I open it to see Tyler, a quiet 7-year-old struggling with a severe stutter, and his parents. Tyler's eyes are downcast, his shoulders hunched. My heart aches for this bright, creative boy trapped inside a body that won't cooperate.

"Hey Tyler, I've got some new art supplies for us to try today," I say gently. Tyler's eyes light up at the sight of the fingerpaints and glitter glue on the table. He plops down and gets to work, tension draining from his small frame.

Over the next hour, we paint, collage, sing, and play. When Tyler relaxes, his speech flows more easily. I celebrate each syllable, each word, praising his hard work. His parents beam with pride.

"Thank you, Emily," his mom says, squeezing my hand. "I can see his confidence growing. You have such a gift for reaching these kids."

Warmth blooms in my chest. Making a difference in young lives - that's why I'm here. My purpose. As I wave goodbye to Tyler, I feel grateful once again for this little town I call home.

I'm chatting with Max as he wipes down tables at the cafe when the bell over the door jingles, announcing a new arrival. I glance up and see Ryan ducking his head to avoid the dangling ferns as he steps inside. A smile tugs at my lips.

"Hey stranger, fancy seeing you here," I call out. Ryan grins and makes his way over.

"Emily, hi! I was hoping I'd run into you," he says. His eyes crinkle at the corners when he smiles. "Want to grab a mug?"

I can't be certain, but I think I see Max wink at me out of the corner of my eye. Trouble maker.

We grab a table in the back, away from the chatter and clinking dishes. The aroma of fresh baked bread and roasted coffee beans wraps around us like a blanket.

"How was your day?" Ryan asks.

I tell him about Tyler's progress. Ryan listens intently, chin resting in his hand. I don't often get to just talk about my passion for speech therapy like this.

Soon we're swapping stories about Ryan's life in the city versus his experiences to date in this sleepy town. The conversation flows easily. For the first time, other than appreciating his very attractive physical appearance, I see Ryan as more than just my colleague. I see the thoughtful, caring man underneath.

"It's nice to connect like this, away from the clinic," Ryan says softly. "I feel like I'm getting to know the real you."

I tuck a strand of hair behind my ear self-consciously. "Same here. We should do this more often." As soon as the words come out of my mouth I wish I could take them back. He might think I'm some kind of maniac who wants to move in with him and force-feed him coffee. Jeepers, Emily. Settle down!

But instead of running away, Ryan nods, his eyes lingering on mine. A new energy hums between us. I take a sip of coffee to steady my suddenly racing heart.

Chapter 6

Ryan

I walk into the brightly lit speech therapy room, taking in the riot of color from educational posters and toys scattered across tables and shelves. Emily greets me with a warm smile, her nurturing spirit evident as she places a reassuring hand on the shoulder of a young boy sitting at a small table. I have to admit I'm quite taken with her delicate features and her smile that radiates confidence and belief in her important work.

"Theo, I'd like you to meet Dr. Mitchell. He's here to help us out today," Emily says gently.

Theo glances up at me shyly through a fringe of sandy hair. I crouch down to his level and offer a friendly handshake. "Nice to meet you, Theo. I hear you've been working real hard with Miss Emily here. I'm just here to lend a hand if I can."

Theo's parents stand off to the side, relief washing over their faces as they see Theo warming to me. I can tell they feel we've got this handled.

Emily pulls up a chair beside Theo. "Alright, let's show the good doctor what we've been practicing!"

I take a seat nearby, watching as Emily delves into a series of speech exercises. She blends encouragement and patience as Theo struggles with certain sounds. When he becomes frustrated, she lightens the mood with a silly joke that draws out his grin. I jot down notes, impressed by her rapport with Theo.

When she looks to me, I provide tidbits of medical insight, like suggesting we strengthen his tongue muscles. Emily beams at the idea. "Excellent thought, Dr. Mitchell!"

Theo's parents relax as we tag team. Our smooth collaboration puts their minds at ease. Before long, Theo makes a breakthrough, clearly enunciating a phrase he's struggled with.

"You did it!" Emily cheers, offering a high-five. Theo's eyes shine with pride. His parents clap, choked up.

I stand and go to them. "Try not to worry. Emily and I will work together to make sure Theo gets the very best care."

Emily joins me and adds warmly, "We've got this covered."

Theo's parents thank us profusely, shaking our hands. As we walk them out, Emily and I share a look. This is the beginning of a great partnership. I can tell we'll make a real difference together while I'm here. Change children's lives for the better.

After Theo's session, Emily and I make our way to the staff lounge. It's a cozy little space, with a round table surrounded by mismatched chairs and walls decorated with clinic flyers and more kids' drawings. There's no shortage of little artists in Sweetwater.

A bulletin board displays notices for various community events, reflecting the close-knit feel here. I can't help but contrast it with the clinical steel fixtures and bare walls at the hospital where I last spent a rotation, the only artwork some garish metal monstrosities gifted by the hospital's wealthy donors, no doubt as some sort of tax write-off.

I take a seat as Emily wipes down the staffroom counter. "That went so well," she says. "Theo responded great to incorporating those oral motor exercises you suggested."

"I was really impressed with how you engaged him," I reply. "You have a real gift for connecting with kids."

Emily smiles as she joins me at the table. "Thanks. I just try to make therapy fun while sneaking in the learning."

We launch into an animated discussion about Theo, exchanging observations and ideas. Emily outlines her plan to target his specific problem sounds through interactive games and repetition. I suggest trying singing as well to get him producing sounds more melodically.

"That's brilliant!" Emily says, scribbling notes. "I can't believe I didn't think of that."

I grin. "Well, you're bringing plenty of great ideas to the table, too. It's been amazing seeing your techniques in action."

We go back and forth, blending our perspectives into an integrated approach. Emily's specialty with engaging young patients complements my medical knowledge. It feels great to collaborate with someone so skilled and passionate.

At one point, we detour into swapping funny stories about our early clinic mishaps, laughing together. The conversation flows easily, both of us enjoying the chance to talk shop.

As we wrap up, Emily smiles warmly. "I think this is the beginning of a beautiful partnership."

I return the smile. "Couldn't agree more."

"Well, I don't know about you, but I could use a real cup of coffee after that session," I say, stretching my arms over my head.

Emily nods enthusiastically. "I was just thinking the same thing! There's a great little cafe just down the street that has the best lattes if you want something fancy. Although Max does a great regular coffee dolloped with whipped cream and a smattering of demerara."

"Perfect. It's been too long since I've had a really good latte," I reply as we gather our things. "Although I'm down to try the other thing you mentioned, too."

We head out into the warm afternoon sunlight. The sidewalks are dotted with people running errands or soaking up the sunny day. Emily and I chat casually as we walk, admiring colorful flower boxes in front of the shops and quaint storefronts.

When we arrive at the cafe, I hold the door for Emily. The aroma of roasted coffee beans envelops us instantly. Local artwork decorates the brick walls, and every table is full of patrons chatting and typing on laptops.

We get in line. Emily recommends the cafe's signature offering - a vanilla latte. I decide to try it along with a slice of cinnamon coffee cake. We find a small table by the front window looking out at the street.

"So what brought you to a small town like this anyway?" Emily asks after we sit down with our coffees. "Did you get a choice about where you went on your rotation?"

"They asked us for our preferences and said they'd be taken into account, but I don't know if they actually care where we want to go. That said, this wouldn't have been my last choice by any means." I launch into the story of how I wanted to get away from the big city hospital scene and try something a little different before I finalize my residency and settle down somewhere and establish my own practice. Emily nods knowingly as I describe wanting to really get to know my patients in a smaller community. "It's just such a different style of medicine, you know?"

In turn, she tells me about growing up here and never wanting to leave. "Sometimes I wonder if I'm keeping my world too small, but I just have everything I need right here and I know I'm making a difference." I find myself captivated by the passion in her voice as she describes the town's charms. Under the informal cafe setting, our conversation shifts to personal details about our lives and interests beyond work.

I discover we share a love of hiking and reading historical fiction. We spend over an hour chatting and laughing. For the first time in a while, I feel fully immersed in the moment, enjoying the company. I'm not checking my phone or my watch, not worrying about working my way through an ever-growing to-do list.

As we get up to leave, Emily turns to me with a warm smile. "We'll have to do this again sometime soon!"

I smile back. "Absolutely. It's a date!" As the words leave my mouth, I realize I wouldn't be opposed to a real date with the beautiful, very impressive Emily.

Chapter 7

Emily

I walk into the therapy room, the familiar smell of crayons and play-doh washing over me. Ryan is already there, arranging colorful blocks and puzzles on the child-sized table. I give him a smile as I hang up my sweater and roll up my sleeves, getting ready to work. I think he secretly likes my workspace the most, because I get to play with fun things like glitter and xylophones rather than stethoscopes and speculums.

The door opens and Theo barrels in, making a beeline for the toy bin. His parents follow behind, greeting us warmly but unable to disguise the worry in their eyes. For some reason, some aspects of his speech have relapsed and they're worried without some intense sessions he'll go back to where he started.

"Hey Theo, wanna show me how your sounds are coming along?" I ask gently. His face falls and he shakes his head, suddenly interested in lining up his trains. I exchange a knowing look with Ryan. Time to tag team this.

Ryan casually grabs the train Theo is clutching and makes choo-choo noises as he rolls it along the table. Theo can't help but giggle. I swoop in next to him with a puppy puppet. "Can you help puppy make his barking sound? Arf arf!" Theo shakes his head again, but there's a hint of a smile now.

I like witnessing this side of Ryan. He's letting me do my thing, not trying to swoop in because he has the fancy degree.

We spend the next half hour prodding, encouraging, distracting and rewarding. Ryan makes silly voices and dances around to get Theo engaged, while I sit close, patiently working on each sound. I can feel his parents' anxious energy behind us, willing Theo to have a breakthrough.

And then it happens. I hold up a picture of a cat and Theo clearly sounds out "c-a-t". A shocked silence, and then an eruption of cheers and praise. Theo laughs with delight, caught up in the celebration. His mom actually has tears in her eyes. "You both have been incredible with Theo. We can't thank you enough!" she gushes.

Ryan grins at me. "We make a great team. Your approach really made the difference today." His praise makes me flush with pride. As Theo's parents usher him out, still reveling in his achievement, Ryan and I share a special smile. This is why we do what we do.

After the high of Theo's breakthrough, I'm ready for some fresh air. "Want to take a walk by the lake?" I ask Ryan. "It's so nice out."

He agrees and we head out past the edge of town, to the walking path that winds along the shoreline. It really is a pretty spot - the water sparkling under the sun, trees swaying in the breeze. A pair of ducks paddle by as we amble along.

"Days like this I remember why I never want to leave this place," I say with a contented sigh. "The peacefulness just seeps into your soul."

Ryan nods. "I definitely fancied myself as more of a city slicker than a country boy. I can't imagine having grown up on a ranch or something, where wide open spaces were my whole world. I'm used to cookie cutter cul-de-sacs and concrete jungles, but this is becoming much more my speed. I really do get the appeal of small town life."

We chat about our childhoods and the paths that led us to this very moment. I share how it was always my dream to help kids like Theo find their voice. Ryan tells me he chose medicine for the puzzle-solving aspect - figuring out how to overcome each patient's unique challenges. It turns out he contemplated audiology as a potential specialty, but ultimately chose to become a general practitioner so he could assist patients with a wide range of ailments.

As the path loops us back around, I pause by a willow tree dipping its branches into the water. "I always find peace here by the lake," I say. "It's where I come to think and dream."

Ryan gazes out across the shimmering water. "It's beautiful. Makes me realize there's more to life than just work and ambition. Financial bonuses are nice, but they don't make you feel like this."

I love seeing this reflective side of him. Our walk has brought us closer, bridging the gap between colleagues and...friends, maybe. The possibilities feel fresh and open.

"You know, I'm getting pretty hungry," Ryan says, turning to me with a smile. "Want to grab some dinner? There's this great little place in town I think you'd love."

My heart flutters at the invitation. "I'd love to! Lead the way."

We drive into town, windows down, country music playing softly.

He takes me to a charming restaurant tucked away on a side street. It's one of the only upscale dining places in town, and it's been a while since I've been here. I haven't been on any dates since my breakup, and I'm not one to go for dinner myself in a place like this. You're much more likely to find me perched on a barstool at Max's cafe grabbing some comfort food.

Fairy lights twinkle around the entrance as Ryan holds the door for me.

Inside, the dining room is intimate yet cozy - just a dozen or so tables with flickering candles and fresh flowers. The chalkboard menu lists local, seasonal dishes like pan-seared trout and braised short ribs with roasted vegetables. My mouth waters just reading it.

We're seated at a small corner table, perfect for private conversation. Ryan orders a bottle of wine and I relax into my chair, thrilled at this unexpected turn. Over appetizers I tell him about my close friendship with Sarah, the local schoolteacher, who's been my rock through every up and down.

When our entrees arrive, he confesses his difficulty opening up to other people, including in past relationships. But with me, he says, it feels natural to share his thoughts and dreams. The candlelight softens his face as he speaks. I'm a little thrown by his casual mention of other relationships, as if he's implying we're in one. But at the same time, the thought doesn't scare me like it normally would. I don't feel pressured. With him, it feels easy. Effortless. And also exciting.

"I'm glad we're doing this, Ryan," I tell him. "It feels like the start of something...special."

He reaches across the table and squeezes my hand. "I think so, too."

His touch makes my hand tingle, a little spindle of electricity working its way up my arm.

It feels like this dinner marks some kind of a turning point, our relationship transitioning from casual acquaintance to real connection. The possibilities feel endless. I'm giddy inside, and I notice he can't stop smiling, either.

Chapter 8

Ryan

The smell of funnel cake and barbecue fills my nose as Emily and I make our way through the crowded fairgrounds. I've come to learn that this annual summer fair is the highlight of the year in our little town, bringing everyone together to celebrate community and enjoy good food, music, and each other's company.

It's all any of my patients have been able to talk about in the weeks leading up to the event. Pumpkin pie this, moonshine that. Even I've found myself getting excited about it. If only my cousin Alex could see me now. He'd roll his eyes so hard at this person I've become.

Emily's eyes light up when she spots Sarah across the way. Her best friend waves enthusiastically and rushes over to greet us.

"Well hey there, you two! Fancy seeing y'all here together," Sarah says with a playful grin. Emily blushes slightly and gives Sarah a knowing look. It doesn't take a genius to know they've been talking about me.

As we continue mingling, I catch whispers and glances in our direction. Word sure travels fast in a small town. I don't mind though. Being here with Emily just feels right. Let them talk!

We run into Max, who claps me on the shoulder. "Seems you're becoming quite the fixture around here these days, 'specially with Miss Emily by your side," he says with a wink.

I didn't know about this guy at first, so friendly and charming. I thought he had a bit of a thing for Emily, but I soon learned their relationship is more like siblings, having grown up next door to each other in Sweetwater.

He's a really nice guy just trying to make a living with his cute little cafe that makes the best scones and lattes in the town.

Emily smiles shyly. "Aw, Ryan's been a great help at the clinic and around town. It's so inspiring to have a doctor of his caliber by my side."

I meet her gaze and smile back warmly. "Happy to lend a hand wherever I can."

Emily loops her arm through mine and steers me towards the food stalls. "C'mon, let me introduce you to some more good folks."

As we make the rounds, Emily is greeted like family. These people clearly adore her. Watching her connect with everyone, I'm really starting to feel like I could call this town home too. With Emily by my side, it already feels more like home than anywhere I've ever been.

Emily and I eventually make our way to the edge of the fairgrounds, seeking a moment of quiet away from the hustle and bustle. We find a secluded spot under a canopy of trees, the distant sound of music and laughter fading into the background.

Above us, the inky night sky glitters with stars. Out here, away from the festival lights, the heavens seem boundless.

"It's beautiful out here, isn't it?" Emily says softly. "Really makes you appreciate the moment."

"Yeah, it's something else," I reply, my eyes fixed on the glittering expanse.

I feel Emily's hand gently brush against mine. The brief contact sends a spark through me. Before I can think twice, I reach out and take her hand in mine.

Emily doesn't pull away. Instead, she interlaces her fingers with mine. I turn to face her. The starlight catches in her eyes like diamonds.

Without exchanging a word, I draw her close. She melts into my embrace. Under the stars, we share a perfect, lingering kiss. Her lips are soft and pillowy, even better than how I imagined them in my dreams.

In this moment, nothing else exists but the two of us. The rest of the world has fallen away.

As we finally break the kiss and I gaze into Emily's eyes again, I know my life will never be the same. She has changed everything.

I head home after the fair with my mind spinning. That kiss with Emily has left me reeling. As I let myself into my apartment, I can't stop thinking about the feel of her lips on mine, the scent of her hair, the warmth of her body against me.

I pace around my living room, running my hands through my hair. These growing feelings for Emily have caught me completely off guard. When I first came to this little town, romance was the furthest thing from my mind. I was focused solely on my job at the clinic, keeping my head down and avoiding attachments. All I planned to do here was count down the days until my residency was over and I could return to the big city where I figured I'd spend the rest of my life.

But Emily has turned all that upside down. Spending time with her these past weeks has awakened something in me I thought was long buried. The more I'm with her, the more I want to be with her. And the small town charm of Sweetwater and its residents is icing on the cake.

What does this mean for my plans? I've never let a relationship get in the way of my goals before. But Emily somehow makes me want to throw caution to the wind and take a chance.

With a sigh, I sink down onto my couch. So many conflicting emotions are running through me - excitement, vulnerability, uncertainty. I know getting involved with Emily would be complicated. This town already feels like home to her in a way I'm not sure it ever could for me. To some degree, I'll always be an outsider compared to the good folks who grew up here.

And I'd be giving up a lot career-wise. I can hear Alex's voice in my head, telling me that living somewhere like this would be settling for someone like me. "You paid for medical school for *this*?" he'd say.

Can I really open myself up to her, not knowing what the future may hold? My heart says to take the leap, but my head urges caution.

I may not have been here for long, but Emily is changing everything I thought I knew about myself.

I just hope we're ready for where this unexpected journey may lead.

Chapter 9

Emily

The canopy of trees parts and I'm greeted by a stunning vista of rolling green hills dotted with wildflowers. Ryan lets out an appreciative whistle as we reach the scenic overlook.

"Well, would you look at that," I smile. "I've lived here my whole life and I never get tired of this view."

He nods, breathing in the fresh mountain air. "It's beautiful. I can see why this trail is so popular."

We stand in comfortable silence for a moment, taking in the landscape spread out before us. I sneak a glance at Ryan's profile, his eyes crinkled at the corners as he smiles softly. Our hands brush and I feel a spark of electricity.

"You know, I didn't peg you for the hiking type when we first met," Ryan says, turning towards me with a playful glint in his eyes. "Little miss fancy speech therapist in her even fancier shoes out on the trail."

I laugh, giving him a light shove. "Oh hush. Just because I wear heels at the clinic doesn't mean I don't know my way around nature." I glance down at my trainers. "In fact, you might be surprised to learn I'm actually a bit of a sneakerhead."

"Is that right?" He grins. "Well consider me schooled. Though I suppose I shouldn't be surprised. You're just full of delightful mysteries, aren't you?"

"Yes sir, this town and I both. More than meets the eye." I wink, feeling emboldened by our easy banter.

Ryan chuckles, a low rumble that makes my heart skip. Our eyes meet and in them I see a new warmth, an unspoken acknowledgement. I know then that something between us has shifted. We've both stopped trying to hide how we feel.

"Emily..." Ryan says softly, turning his body to face me fully. Our eyes lock and in them I see a vulnerability and tenderness that makes my breath catch.

"Yeah?" I whisper.

"I didn't expect to feel this way about someone. Especially not here." He reaches up and brushes a strand of hair from my face, his touch igniting sparks along my skin. "But you...you're different. Special."

My heart pounds in my chest. "Ryan, I..."

He moves closer, our faces just inches apart. "Tell me if I'm wrong here."

I shake my head, words failing me. He leans in and then his lips capture mine in the sweetest, gentlest kiss. My hands come up, fingers curling into his shirt as our mouths move together. It's perfect, even better than the first.

When we finally pull back, foreheads touching, I let out a shaky laugh. "Well, ain't you just full of surprises too."

Ryan smiles, caressing my cheek. "I'm glad we found each other, Emily."

"Me too," I whisper, before drawing him into another kiss under the setting sun. Here, on this mountain, we mark the start of something beautiful between us. And my heart feels fuller than it's ever been.

I'm still floating on a cloud as I make my way to Max's cafe on Main Street. He looks up with a grin as the bell above the door announces my arrival.

"Well hey there, sunshine," Max says, already grabbing two mugs from behind the counter. "I was just about to close up but I got time for you. What'll it be, the usual?"

I slide onto a stool at the counter, unable to keep the smile off my face. "That'd be perfect, thanks Max."

He raises an eyebrow at me but doesn't say anything as he starts preparing the whipped cream for our coffees. I trace little patterns on the worn countertop, thinking about the feeling of Ryan's lips on mine.

"So..." Max says slowly. "Either you won the lottery, or something happened on that hike with Ryan."

I look up to find him watching me closely. I should've known I wouldn't be able to hide anything from him.

"We kissed again," I confess, feeling myself flush. "It just happened so naturally, like we'd been building up to that moment."

Max lets out a low whistle. "Well, it's about damn time if you ask me. I've seen the way that boy looks at you."

He tops the coffees with whipped cream and demerara and brings them over to sit beside me. I wrap my hands around the warm mug, comforted by its familiarity.

"I really like him, Max." I bite my lip. "But I'm a little scared too. What if it doesn't work out?"

Max reaches out and squeezes my hand. "Now don't go borrowing trouble, Em. Just take it one step at a time and see where it goes. You deserve a little romance, just like anyone else."

I nod slowly. He's right - I can't let fear hold me back.

"What about you, Max? Seeing anyone lately?" I try to divert the conversation by redirecting It to Max's love life, always a source of amusing tales of Tinder dates gone wrong in neighboring towns.

"No, no. We're not doing that today. Today the focus is on you and that lover boy of yours. Dr. Ryan." Max makes a kissy face.

I blush.

"Emily, the thing is... sometimes you just gotta take that leap of faith," Max says gently. "I got a feelin' this could be the real thing for you. And real love - that's worth the risk."

I lean over to kiss his freckled cheek. "Thanks, Max. You always know just what to say."

With his encouragement ringing in my ears, I feel ready to embrace this new chapter with Ryan. Whatever comes next, we'll figure it out together.

Ryan

I'm sorting through clean clothes in my hamper and getting ready for bed when my phone rings. It's Alex.

"Hey stranger, long time no chat!" I say, settling onto the couch. Sleep can wait. I really have missed this guy. We used to do basically everything together back in the big city.

"Hey Ryan, how's my favorite small town boy?" Alex's voice crackles over the line. "Still living the quiet life?"

I laugh. "It's not as quiet as you think. I've actually got some big news..."

I proceed to tell Alex all about Emily - how we met, our hike earlier, the kiss under the sunset. Saying it out loud makes my heart flutter all over again.

"Wow, congrats man! She sounds great," Alex says sincerely. "But just make sure you're being smart here. Don't do anything to jeopardize your plans."

I furrow my brow, confused by his tone. "What do you mean?"

"I just want you to keep your eye on the prize. We always said we'd make something amazing out of ourselves. Be the great successes that we have the potential to be. For you, that means being one of the best doctors in this city. Don't let a girl derail that."

I bristle slightly. "Alex, I'm not just going to drop my goals. But I really care about Emily. I'm not sure why you don't think I can balance both."

Alex sighs. "I'm not saying you can't. Just remember what's important, that's all." An edge creeps into his voice. "You've always been a dreamer, Ryan. Don't lose sight of the bigger picture."

I bite my tongue, holding back a sharp retort. Something about his words is rubbing me the wrong way. He's right, though. His goals and mine have always been very closely aligned.

We chat a few more minutes about innocuous topics before I make an excuse to get off the phone.

As I crawl into bed, Alex's words swirl around my mind. I know he means well, but he just doesn't understand. Things change. It's part of life. My dreams are starting to be here in this town and now include Emily. And her encouragement today makes me believe more than ever that maybe I really can have it all - love, community, and success.

I can't and won't let Alex or anyone else make me question that. With Emily by my side, I feel like I can take on the whole world.

Chapter 10

Emily

The scent of fresh bread and jam draws me through the bustling farmers' market. Vendors call out specials on plump tomatoes and sweet corn as I weave between stands overflowing with the season's bounty.

"Try a sample of my homemade blueberry jam, dear," Betty Sue offers, holding out a tiny spoon. She's a dear old woman known for her colorful, frilly aprons and her unbeatable preserves. Nobody even tries to go up against her in the town't annual jam-making contest anymore, because nobody holds a candle to her.

The sweet tang bursts over my tongue. "Mmm, that's delicious. You've really captured the essence of summer."

Betty Sue beams. "Why thank you! I'm so glad you like it."

I turn to Ryan with a smile. "I love these little moments in our town. It's like time slows down so you can really savor things."

Ryan grins back at me as we continue wandering the lively market, chatting with the friendly vendors who've known me since I was knee-high. There's a warmth here, a way folks really see you.

We meander next door to Happily Ever After, the cozy bookshop run by Mrs. Clara, a bookish widow who takes great pleasure in matching everyone who enters the store with their favorite book. The faint smell of dusty pages wraps around me like an old friend as we browse the overflowing shelves.

Ryan plucks out a familiar title.

"I didn't know you were a fan of H.D. Carlton. I love her work, too!"

"Oh yes, I adore her writing! The way she captures the essence of healthy relationships is so beautiful." I launch eagerly into my favorite passages and characters, thrilled to find someone who shares this literary love.

Ryan hangs on my every word as I talk about some of my other favorite authors, interjecting his own thoughts on their evocative descriptions of love, relationships and, occasionally, Southern living. Our conversation flows effortlessly, two minds in sync. With him, it feels like coming home.

After leaving the bookshop, we head to Magnolia Park. The sprawling oaks offer pockets of shade from the afternoon sun as we spread out our picnic blanket. I unpack the sandwiches and potato salad I whipped up this morning, while Ryan produces two cold bottles of Cheerwine.

"I brought a frisbee too, if you're up for it after we eat," he says, his boyish grin making my heart flutter.

I take a bite of my pimiento cheese sandwich and sigh contentedly. "This is perfect. I love how peaceful it is here."

"You know, I'd never even tried pimiento cheese until I moved to Sweetwater, and now I just can't get enough," Ryan says between bites. "A bit like how I feel about you," he adds, causing me to blush.

We chat lightly as we eat, shoulders brushing, the playful breeze catching strands of my hair. When we finish, Ryan jumps up and grabs the frisbee, his athletic frame limber and enthusiastic. I squeal as I run after his first throw, the red disc cutting through the air.

He injects an unexpected playfulness into my life, one I thought I'd left behind in childhood.

After tiring ourselves out, we meander hand-in-hand along the wooded trails, sunlight dappling through the leaves. Ryan points out birds and stops to examine curious mushrooms and plants. His curiosity about nature reminds me of my own innate wonder about the world. "For a city boy you sure know a lot about nature," I tease.

"I knew one day my time in Eagle Scouts would come in handy," he grins back. "You should see what I can do with a length of rope."

As the sun begins its lazy descent, we make our way back through town. My little blue house comes into view, the porch swing Ryan fixed last week swaying gently. "You're pretty handy for a city boy, too."

"I am pretty good with my hands," he grins, making me blush for what feels like the hundredth time today.

I turn to him, suddenly shy. "Would you like to come in for some sweet tea?" The question hangs between us, weighted with possibility. His eyes meet mine, deep and unwavering.

"I'd love to."

I lead Ryan through the front door of my house, the familiar creak of the hinges and scent of lavender potpourri welcoming us home. I gesture for him to have a seat on the plush sofa while I busy myself in the kitchen, pouring two tall glasses of sweet tea over ice. I slice up a lemon and drop a piece into each glass along with a sprig of fresh mint.

When I return to the living room, I notice Ryan admiring the framed photos on the mantle - my parents smiling on their wedding day, my niece and nephew grinning with missing teeth, the town fair from years past.

"It looks like you have so many great memories here," he says.

"I do. This town has been my whole world. My siblings up and left but I couldn't bring myself to do it, so I live vicariously through their stories, and now yours." I sit next to him on the sofa, acutely aware of his nearness. "What about you? Where did you grow up?"

As we talk, inching closer together, I'm amazed by how comfortable and natural it feels, like we're two threads woven into the same tapestry.

When a lull finally falls in the conversation, the air seems to crackle between us. Ryan reaches out and brushes a strand of hair from my face, his fingers leaving a trail of sparks on my skin.

"Emily, you are so beautiful, inside and out," he says softly.

I lean in closer, heart hammering. "So are you," I whisper.

And then his lips meet mine, tentative at first, then hungry and insistent. My hands tangle in his hair as the kiss deepens, both of us having wanted this for so long.

We come up for air, foreheads touching. "I didn't want to rush this, to mess it up," Ryan murmurs.

"Me neither, but it feels right, doesn't it?"

He answers by pulling me back to him, our bodies fitting together like two puzzle pieces. I lead him wordlessly to my bedroom as we shed our clothes piece by piece.

We take our time exploring each other, whispering affectionate words and learning what makes the other gasp with pleasure. It's unlike any other encounter I've had - it feels like making love.

Afterwards, we lie peacefully tangled together, skin against skin, our bodies sheened with sweat. The setting sun casts everything in a warm glow as we talk and laugh softly, voices hushed in the intimacy of this moment.

"I've never felt as known by someone as I do by you," I confess, tracing patterns on his chest. "That felt so right. Being with you feels so right."

Ryan kisses the top of my head. "I've been lost for a long time, but you really do make me feel found, Miss Emily."

As we drift off to sleep, limbs entwined, my heart is full of hope for the love we've found in this little corner of the world.

I wake wrapped in Ryan's arms, blinking in the early morning sunlight streaming through my bedroom window. For a moment I just watch him sleep, his features soft and relaxed, his hair endearingly mussed. My heart swells looking at him there beside me.

If you'd told me mere months ago that I'd fall in love with the new doctor in town I would have laughed, because it just seemed so unlikely. Yet, here we are, and I couldn't imagine life being any other way.

As I shift, he stirs and pulls me closer. "Mornin'," he mumbles, voice gravelly with sleep.

"Morning," I say softly, nestling into him.

We lay there for a little while longer, neither inclined to move just yet. I sigh contentedly. "I could get used to this." For a moment, my stomach drops. Goodness. What if my words scare him away?

Ryan kisses my shoulder. "I was thinking the same thing."

My stomach rumbles then, and we both laugh.

"I suppose we should get some breakfast," Ryan says.

"Mm, probably a good idea." I stretch and reluctantly slip from the tangle of sheets. Ryan follows me from the bedroom, both of us pulling on enough clothing for decency's sake. In a small town like this, everybody's always glancing through the windows as they go by.

In the kitchen, we work in tandem - Ryan scrambling eggs while I set the table and put on coffee. Domestic bliss.

Over breakfast on my little balcony, looking out on the neighborhood just beginning to wake, we talk about our plans for the day, then the week, and then the future. It all feels so natural, being with him like this.

My heart is full of hope for the growing love we've found.

Chapter 11

Emily

I pull up to Sarah's quaint blue cottage, the one she's lived in since we were kids. It's a refuge, a sanctuary. Just what I need right now.

I step onto the creaky front porch and pause to breathe in the scent of lavender and roses from her garden. Through the front window, I can see Sarah flitting around the cozy living room, lighting candles and plumping pillows.

She opens the round wooden door before I knock, sweeping me into a hug. "Emily! I've been waiting for you all day."

I follow her inside, comforted by the familiar art and furnishings that make this place so uniquely Sarah. We settle onto the plush sofa with mugs of chamomile tea, tucked beneath a hand-crocheted blanket.

"Thanks for having me over, Sare. I just...I needed to talk."

She nods, her kind eyes searching mine. "Of course, honey. What's on your mind?"

I stare into my tea, watching the steam curl up in wisps. "It's Ryan. I can't stop thinking about him leaving after his residency. My heart says dive in, but my head screams to pump the brakes. His time in Sweetwater was never going to be forever, and I'm having a hard time thinking about him leaving."

Sarah reaches over to squeeze my hand, a sad smile on her lips. "Oh Em, I know it's scary. But bottling up your feelings won't do you any good. You need to tell that boy how you really feel."

My throat tightens. "But what if he doesn't feel the same way? What if I spill my guts and he leaves anyway? And I don't want to take him away from his dreams. He has so much potential, and he can't achieve all of that here. He just can't."

"Then at least you'll know, darlin'. Walking around in limbo is no way to live."

I let out a shaky breath. She's right. Ryan at least deserves to know the truth so he can weigh things up and make an informed decision about his future. And that way, I'll get to find out how he truly feels about me. That I'm not just going to become some small town story he can laugh about with his big city friends when he returns.

"You're absolutely right, Sare. I owe it to both of us to lay all my cards on the table."

Sarah grins. "There's my brave girl."

Ryan

I'm pacing around my apartment, phone pressed to my ear as the voice on the other end delivers unexpected and life-changing news.

"Thank you, this is an incredible opportunity," I say, my brow furrowed. "I just need some time to think about it."

I end the call and rake a hand through my hair. A prestigious hospital in the city just offered me a lucrative position doing cutting-edge medicine. This is everything I've worked toward. The opportunity would throw my general practitioner goals out the window, but in the face of the money and all the other perks that come with a job like this, I'm compelled to take it.

But then my thoughts drift to Emily. We've grown so close these past months. I can't imagine leaving her and this quaint town I've come to love. Cutting my residency short wasn't something I thought would be possible.

I sink onto the edge of my bed, the old springs creaking beneath me. My mind is spinning with indecision. Do I follow my career ambitions that have driven me all these years? Or do I give it all up for a chance at love in this sleepy town?

I glance around at the bare walls and sparse furniture. This was always meant to be temporary. I never expected to put down roots here.

But Emily makes me imagine a different kind of life. Lazy mornings on the porch, familiar faces at the diner, Friday nights at the local honky tonk. A simpler life, but a full one.

My heart and my head wage war as I agonize over my choice. The opportunity could launch my career to new heights. But Emily has awakened something in me I thought long buried - a longing for a home like I never thought I'd have.

I rake my hands down my face and sigh. I need to see Emily. We have some hard conversations ahead.

I take a deep breath as I push open the door to the diner, the familiar bells jangling above me. I spot Emily tucked into our usual booth by the window, backlit by the setting sun. Even in her work scrubs with her hair pulled back, she looks beautiful.

My heart leaps at the sight of her, then sinks again with uncertainty. I slide into the booth across from her.

"Hey," I say with a tentative smile.

"Hi." She fiddles with the napkin in front of her, not quite meeting my eyes. An uneasy silence settles between us.

Finally I break it. "So a hospital in the city called me yesterday..."

Emily's eyes snap to mine, apprehension written on her face. "Oh yeah? What did they say?"

I rub the back of my neck, avoiding her gaze. "Well, it was very unexpected..."

A shadow passes over her face, like she's anticipating what I'm about to say.

I take a deep breath. "They offered me a position. A really prestigious one, with access to state-of-the-art equipment and leading research."

I chance a look at Emily. She's staring down at the table, shoulders slumped.

"That's...that's great, Ryan," she says faintly. "Congratulations." The word comes out of her mouth with the energy of a slug on Benadryl.

"Yeah, it's an amazing opportunity." I let out a long breath. "But it would mean leaving Sweetwater. Leaving you."

Emily looks up at me, eyes glistening. "What are you saying?"

My heart pounds. This is it - the moment that will define my future.

"I'm saying..." I reach across the table and take her hand in mine. "I'm considering staying. If you'll have me. Or maybe you can come with me. I don't know. All I know is I'm confused and I don't want this to end."

A brilliant smile breaks across Emily's face. She squeezes my hand, joy and relief mingling on her features. No words needed. But just as quickly it fades. "I could never leave Sweetwater, Ryan. And I don't wnat you to give up on your dreams."

Her words hit me with their sincerity, with their selflessness. In that moment I know - my heart has won. But that might mean leaving. And as Emily gazes at me from across that greasy diner table, I've never felt more at home. At least for now. I have some decisions to make.

Chapter 12

Ryan

I pace the length of my cramped living room, phone in hand. My small apartment feels like a cage tonight, the peeling wallpaper and thrift store furniture mocking me. I need to talk this through with someone removed from the situation.

Someone who knows me well, who can provide an objective opinion without the smothering force of Sweetwater and the way its charm seems to lure me in.

Someone who's not Emily.

I tap Alex's name and he pops up onscreen, his sleek highrise condo glittering behind him. "Hey cuz, what's up?"

I sink onto the lumpy couch. "I got offered a job at County General. Head of their new division exploring advanced medicine... the same area I focused on during my first residency rotation."

Alex whistles. "Damn, look at you moving up in the world! That's huge, congrats! When do you get the heck out of the boonies?"

I nod, but can't meet his eyes. "Thanks, it is a big deal. It's just...like you said, it would mean leaving town."

"And?" He raises an eyebrow. "You're not getting cold feet are you? This is your shot, Ryan. A stepping stone to bigger things."

My throat tightens. "I know. But I've put down roots here. Made connections." Emily's face flashes in my mind.

Alex snorts. "Connection? Don't tell me this is about some small-town Susie homemaker."

I bristle at his dismissive tone. "Her name's Emily. She's one of the best speech therapists in the state."

"Uh huh. Well here's some tough love, cuz. Ditch the chick and take the job. You'll never get ahead chasing skirts." He leans back, supremely confident in his advice. "This was only ever meant to be a temporary stop for you, anyway."

My hands curl into fists. Who is he to judge Emily without even meeting her? To assume my only reservation is a fleeting romance? I want to argue but he's already moved on, extolling the virtues of city life, as if success is measured in skyscraper views and expense accounts alone. Typical lawyer, I think to myself.

His words sink like stones in my gut. My future hung in the balance, the two paths diverging. But as Alex prattles on, my decision only crystallizes. Emily saw me, not just the white coat and stethoscope.

Saw beyond the traditional trappings of achievement. I can't simply cast that aside.

This is my life, my choice. And despite the cost to my career, I'm seriously considering choosing her.

Emily

I take a deep breath as I push open the door to the cozy cafe, the rich aroma of fresh coffee enveloping me like a warm hug. Max's really is one of my sanctuaries, a refuge from the storms of life. Especially today, as uncertainty churns within me.

Max looks up from wiping down the counter, his kind eyes crinkling with his smile. "Hey Em. The usual?"

I manage a small smile back. "Please." As he busies himself with my whipped cream and demerara coffee, I sink into my favorite armchair in the corner, the overstuffed cushions embracing me.

Max brings over my drink, studying me with concern. "Everything okay, hon? You look like you've got the weight of the world on your shoulders. You're not the giddy schoolgirl who just made out with the hunky young doctor... a far cry from last time you came in."

I sigh, the dam breaking as I confide my worries about Ryan. The words pour out - my fear of falling for someone transient, who could leave at any moment. The job offer potentially cutting his residency short. Max listens patiently, his steady presence soothing me.

"It's risky, getting involved with someone potentially temporary," he says gently. "I know you, Em. You give your whole heart. But sometimes we have to protect it."

I nod, blinking back tears. He's right - I dive in fully, while Ryan's future here is uncertain. I'm an idiot, falling for someone when I promised myself I wouldn't after my last heartbreak.

"But take it slow," Max squeezes my hand. "Don't close yourself off completely. What you two could have may be worth the risk."

I take a shaky sip of coffee, comforted by the frothiness of the whipped cream and the hot brown liquid. Max always knows exactly what to say, his wisdom a light in the fog. The future is unclear, but with friends like him, I know I'll find my way.

The sun filters through the trees, dappling the walking path with light as Ryan and I stroll through the park. But despite the tranquil setting, tension simmers beneath the surface.

We dance around the elephant in the room, making small talk about work and the weather. But the lingering job offer hangs over us, the unspoken words swelling until the dam breaks.

"Emily, we need to talk about this," Ryan finally says.

My shoulders tense. "Talk about what?" I mutter, kicking a pebble. Part of me wants to run away, to do anything but have this conversation.

"You know what," he says gently. "The hospital job. I can tell it's bothering you."

I stop, turning to face him. "Of course it is! You could be leaving any day now. How am I supposed to feel?" The words burst out before I can stop them.

Ryan runs a hand through his hair in frustration. "So you just want me to turn down an amazing opportunity?"

"No, I just..." I trail off helplessly. "I don't know where I fit into your big city plans."

"Emily, we just met. Don't you think you're getting too attached?" He asks bluntly.

I recoil as if stung. "Too attached? I thought we had something special growing between us."

Ryan shakes his head. "This job is a huge deal for my career. I can't just give it up for someone I barely know."

His words hit me like a blow. I thought we were on the same page, but clearly I misread everything.

I blink back furious tears. "Well then, I guess this barely-know-you should stop wasting your time," I choke out, before turning and fleeing the park, his calls echoing after me.

Chapter 13

Ryan

I sit alone in the dim living room, the only light coming from the single lamp in the corner. Shadows dance across the walls, mirroring the unease in my mind. I sigh and rub my temples, thoughts of Emily and this small town swirling.

I'm not proud of my interaction with her earlier. The walk was meant to be a way for us to talk, to share our feelings in a somewhat neutral territory. But all I did was take my confusion out on her. I know I hurt her. Her face right before she ran away will be stamped in my dreams.

The last few months here have been eye-opening. Making real connections, feeling part of a community--it's something I've never experienced before. And Emily...she makes me feel ways I didn't think possible.

I pace to the window, gazing at the quiet streets below. This town has wrapped itself around my heart. But then I turn and see the unopened envelope on the table, my ticket to the career I've always wanted. The official job offer sent through by the hospital.

I sink into the couch, head in hands. "Is this job worth losing what I've found here?" I whisper. "Worth losing Emily?"

My heart and mind wage war as I stare into the shadows. The life I thought I wanted, or this new path filled with meaning. Emily's smile flashes in my mind, and I know--there's no choice to make.

Emily

The moonlight filters through the leaves, casting a silver glow on the garden below. I kneel in the damp soil, the scent of night blooms enveloping me in familiar comfort. My hands work methodically, pruning and weeding, as my troubled thoughts churn.

Even if he doesn't take the unexpected job offer, Ryan's residency is ending soon. He'll be off to his big city hospital, leaving me behind in this sleepy town. I snip a dead flower, bitterness rising in my throat. We both knew this was temporary, but my foolish heart ignored logic.

Sure, he mentioned me potentially going with him. But he probably didn't mean it, and was saying it to placate me. Besides, my life is here. I don't want to move out of Sweetwater, let alone to a big city.

I cradle a drooping bud, strengthening its stem. "I can't let myself get hurt again," I whisper into the night. Other men have breezed into town, made me feel special, then left without a backward glance. "I need to protect my heart."

A firefly lands on my palm, its glow soon fading. Like Ryan's feelings for me, I fear. My breath hitches, but I force the tears back. I am not weak. I am strong, with deep roots in this community.

The wispy leaves nod in the breeze, reminding me - seasons change, but I endure. I will nurture my heart and move forward, even if it means leaving Ryan behind. The garden has taught me growth sometimes requires painful pruning.

I stand, brushing soil from my knees. I can't control Ryan's path, only my own. As the moon guides me inside, I make a silent vow - I will not be a rest stop for wandering men. My heart, my life, are not disposable things. This time, I will protect myself.

Emily

The next morning, I make my way to the cozy cafe where Ryan and I first properly connected over coffee and conversation. The familiar smells of roasted beans and cinnamon surround me, but today it provides little comfort.

Ryan is already seated at a corner table when I arrive, nursing a steaming mug. His shoulders are hunched, eyes downcast. My heart twists, but I steel myself. I cannot let his mood sway my resolve.

Max glances over from the counter, concern etched on his face.

Sliding into the chair across from him, I offer a weak smile. "Hey there," I say softly.

His head jerks up, surprise flickering across his face. "Emily. I wasn't sure you'd come."

I stir sugar into my coffee to avoid meeting his gaze. "I considered staying home today."

An uneasy silence settles between us. I sneak a glance at Ryan. His forehead is creased with worry, his fingers tapping nervously on the tabletop.

Finally he speaks, voice strained. "Emily, I think we need to talk about...this. Us."

I take a shaky breath, clutching my mug like an anchor. "What about us?" I ask quietly.

He runs an agitated hand through his hair. "I just - I'm sorry for how I spoke to you last time we tried to talk about this. But my residency is ending soon, regardless of whether I take this job or not. I'll be leaving. This could never be forever."

There it is. The truth we've danced around for weeks. Hearing him say it out loud makes my chest constrict painfully.

I look him straight in the eyes. "Then I guess this really was only temporary after all and I'm an idiot for thinking I might mean enough to you for you to consider staying."

Ryan flinches. "Emily..." he trails off helplessly.

I stand abruptly, the cafe spinning around me. "I have to go."

As I flee into the golden morning, tears slip down my cheeks. I swipe them away angrily. Some things just aren't meant to last. And a small town girl like me has no place in a big city doctor's future.

Chapter 14

Emily

The bell on the clinic door jingles, and my heart jumps into my throat when I see Ryan walk in. This place was a place I could get out of my own head, filled with giggling children and grateful parents, but his presence casts an uneasy shadow.

"Emily," he says, raking a hand through his tousled brown hair. "Can we talk?"

To be fair, he's tried to have this conversation with me twice now, and I've run away both times. But at least one of those times he's deserved it.

I busy my hands straightening folders on my desk, stalling as I gather my thoughts. "I have a patient coming soon."

"Please," he insists, stepping closer. His faded jeans and flannel shirt look out of place amid the bright colors of the clinic. He weirdly looks more like he fits here in Sweetwater than I do. "Things have been off between us lately. I want to fix this giant elephant in the room so we can both be happy."

My shoulders tense. The hopeful look in his hazel eyes used to make me melt, but now it only reminds me of his indecision about our future.

"Ryan, you know how I feel. I want a life here, but you..." I falter, lowering my voice. "You seem set on leavin' town."

He winces. "It isn't that simple, Emily. I worked my whole life for an opportunity like this, and now everything is suddenly up in the air because I grew feelings for you."

I look away, fussing with a jar of lollipops to avoid his earnest gaze.

"Emily, look at me," he implores, tilting my chin up. "I'm tryin', darlin'. Just give me a little more time."

The endearment nearly breaks my resolve, but I steel myself. "I can't wait forever, Ryan. I have to think about myself too."

He sighs, shoulders slumping. "I understand. I just don't wanna lose you but I have a decision to make and that might end up being the outcome."

We stand in tense silence until the door opens and my next patient skips inside. Ryan touches my arm gently in farewell before slipping out, the unresolved issues hanging thick as the summer humidity. The clinic, typically a refuge, suddenly feels stifling, no longer a shelter from the storm raging in my heart.

I leave the clinic feeling drained, the weight of Ryan's indecision pressing down on me. Needing an empathetic ear, I head to the town library, my footsteps echoing on the creaky wooden floors as I make my way to the fiction section.

There, surrounded by the familiar smell of old books, I find the quirky Lily shelving the new arrivals. Her kind eyes and warm smile immediately put me at ease.

"Hey hon, you look a little down. Everything alright?"

I sigh, leaning against the shelves. "Ryan stopped by the clinic today. He says he wants to work things out between us, but..."

Lily sets down her stack of books, giving me her full attention. "But his being noncommittal is givin' you doubts. He told me about that job offer of his... all the shiny new equipment and fancy patients..."

"Exactly," I say. "I want roots here, marriage and kids someday. But Ryan won't give me a straight answer about his plans. I feel so vulnerable."

Lily nods. "I know it's scary puttin' your heart on the line. But don't let fear stop you from taking a chance on love. Have you told Ryan how you truly feel?"

I shake my head, looking down. "I don't want to pressure him, and every time he tries to talk about it I freak out and run away."

"Oh honey," Lily says gently. "Sometimes you gotta lay it all out, even if you think they know. Make it crystal clear."

I ponder her words in the cozy hush of the library. She's right. If I want Ryan to understand, I have to tell him plainly.

"You've given me a lot to think about," I tell Lily. "Ryan's not the only one with doubts. But being honest is worth the risk."

Lily smiles and pulls me in for a hug. "That's my girl. Y'all will work it out, just have faith."

Leaving the library's calm, serene comfort, I feel ready to bridge the gap between me and Ryan. Lily is right - open communication is the key.

I retreat to my garden after visiting Lily, needing time to gather my thoughts. The late afternoon sun washes over the flower beds as I slowly meander along the gravel paths. Vibrant zinnias and sunflowers dance in the gentle breeze, oblivious to my inner turmoil.

I brush my fingers over the velvety petals of the gardenias I'd planted when I first moved in years ago. Their sweet fragrance never failed to calm me. But today, my mind is too preoccupied to find peace.

All I can think about is Ryan. Our strained interactions over the past weeks replay in my mind. The moments of tension, of things left unsaid. I see the sadness in his eyes that I'm sure mirror my own.

We both cared so deeply, but fear and doubts have built up barriers between us. I want to tear those walls down, to be vulnerable and honest about my feelings. But a small voice holds me back, warning of potential hurt.

Can I really lay my heart bare, when there is no guarantee Ryan will do the same? The thought of putting myself out there so completely fills me with anxiety.

Yet I knew Lily was right. If this relationship has any chance at all, I have to be brave enough to share my true emotions, no matter how difficult.

I kneel down, cupping a perfect rose bloom in my hand. Its petals are so delicate, yet the thorns are sharp. Much like love itself - beautiful but requiring courage.

"Can I let go of my fear for a chance at love?" I whisper. The flowers swayed silently with no answer except the one in my heart. I knew what I need to do.

Ryan

I stand at the window of my apartment, looking out over the quaint main street of this small town I—for now—call home. Emily's clinic—for the past few months, mine too—is just down the block, though I can't see it from this angle.

My mind wanders back to our strained conversation there earlier. I tried to make amends, to let her know I want to make this work. But my indecision about staying has only driven us further apart. Which is fair. I think I'd be acting exactly the same way in her shoes.

I sigh, leaning my forehead against the cool glass. What am I so afraid of? Committing to Emily means committing to this town, to putting down roots when I've always been a wanderer.

But when I imagine leaving, I picture her kind eyes and radiant smile and know they'd haunt me wherever I went. I'll never find another woman like her.

"Am I willing to give up everything I've worked for...for her?" I mutter.

I think of late nights in the office, promotions, sacrificing a personal life for professional success. Is that what I still want? Or am I ready for something real, even if it means changing my whole world?

The choice is terrifying, but suddenly clear. I have to tell Emily how I feel, no matter the risk. I can't lose her because of my own insecurities.

Grabbing my keys, I rush out the door before I can overthink it. I have to find her now, to finally speak from my heart.

It's time to bridge this gap between us, once and for all.

Chapter 15

Emily

If there's one thing that gets everyone excited in Sweetwater, other than speculation about Ryan's and my romantic future, it's an excuse to get dressed up and throw a party. And one of the biggest events of the year is Sweetwater's annual SweetwaterFest, a charity event held at the community center.

I, like most other townspeople, attend every year, and despite the funk I'm in, still committed to helping out so here I am.

Looking around, I think we've done a good job of setting the place up with festive banners and twinkling lights. The event is filled with laughter, music, and a variety of shared activities from pot luck meals and cooking contests to karaoke.

I do my best to keep my mind distracted, busying myself with organizing decorations, and later throwing myself into conversations with folk known for their ability to chat away on any topic. All of these diversion tactics enable me to do what I intend to for the duration of the event: stay as far away from Dr. Ryan Mitchell as humanly possible.

Initially, my stalling tactic works well and I only catch brief glimpses of him as he walks by helping people to carry heavy items from one side of the center to the other in preparation for the bash.

"Emily, Ryan, could you two handle the auction? We need all hands on deck." My heart lurches in my chest as Sissy Darlington's voice rings out across the arts and crafts table that I'm switching over for the next group of budding artists.

Great. Just what I was trying to avoid.

"Oh, you don't want me to keep doing this?" I stall, gesturing at the table before me with its glitter and paper punches and crayons. Anyone can see the table is more than ready to go, and Sissy is no exception. She places a hand on her hip, clipboard held firmly in the other, and gives me a strange look.

"Emily, please. Roger has sprained his ankle and Glenys is helping him. The auction is the most important part of the event and we need a reliable pair to pull this off."

I glance over at Ryan who's standing to the other side of Sissy looking just as apprehensive. I sigh. "Okay, I'd be more than happy to help, Sissy. Show us what you need."

Unfortunately, this means I have to work side by side with Ryan for the next two hours.

We begin arranging the auction items on the central table, hyper-aware of each other but not exchanging a word. A bead of sweat drips down my back as I carefully set down Miss Betty's famous peach pie. The sounds of the band striking up a lively tune and the delighted shrieks of children seem to mock the roiling unease within me.

Because of the excitement around the auction, it also means we don't really have to talk to each other at first, except for courteous murmurs as we step around each other carefully and try to avoid Roger's fate.

Finally, the auction successfully run, we find ourselves alone. And it's time to have the conversation I've been running away from for far too long.

Ryan

Finally, I clear my throat. "Emily, can we talk for a minute?" I ask quietly. The twinkling lights and happy chatter around us feels miles away from the tension brewing between us.

She pauses, then nods, stepping closer. The floral scent of her perfume envelops me.

"I know things have been...strained between us," I begin hesitantly. "But I want you to know, you're a huge priority for me. I'm just trying to figure things out."

I lead her outside into a quieter area. The strings of lights cast a soft glow over the community garden, removed from the bustle of the event inside. Emily and I find ourselves alone out here, the distant hum of the crowd barely audible.

Emily's arms are crossed, her posture tense. I know this conversation won't be easy, but it's one we need to have. Even in her apprehension, she's breathtaking.

"Ryan, I'm tired of feeling like I'm last on your priority list. You say you want a future with me, but you might be leaving now. You're definitely leaving at some point. And my future is here in Sweetwater. I can't keep going along in this limbo," Emily says, her voice strained.

I sigh, running my hand through my hair. "That's not true..." I say, but my words don't even run true to me. "Look, I know there's been a lot to think about, and our future together is on the line. We should talk about it."

Emily shakes her head, eyes glistening. "There is no 'our future.' You're chasing your dreams halfway across the country while I'm left here picking up the pieces."

"So you expect me to give up everything I've worked for?" I ask defensively.

"No, I want you to include me in your plans. To consider me, us, in your dreams," she pleads.

I soften, realizing how my singular focus has hurt her. "You're right, I've been selfish. My dreams mean nothing without you in them. And not letting you in, to understand all the things I've been considering, and to not let you know how I truly feel, was wrong of me."

I take her hand tentatively. The string lights flicker, matching the uncertainty in her eyes. Have I left too much unsaid between us? Can we move forward together? The garden is serene, but our hearts are in turmoil.

I take a deep breath as we stand together under the canopy of stars, the distant sounds of the event fading away. Emily's hand feels small and delicate in mine, yet distant, as if she could pull away at any moment.

"Emily, I know I've made mistakes, been too focused on my work and future plans and it might have felt like I've done it without considering you," I say gently.

She nods, unshed tears glistening in her eyes. "I've felt so alone recently, like you have one foot out the door."

My heart aches, hating that I've made her feel that way. "I'm sorry I ever made you doubt me, doubt us. You're the most important thing in my world."

Emily looks up at me searchingly. "Then why does it feel like you're always looking ahead to the next chapter of your life, one I'm not part of?"

I squeeze her hand, willing her to feel my sincerity. "I want you by my side in every chapter, Em. I've just been terrible at showing it."

She sighs, the hurt still evident on her face. "I don't know if I can keep waiting for you to include me in your plans, Ryan."

The fear of losing her hits me like a punch to the gut. Under the peaceful night sky, I know I have to make a choice - keep chasing my dreams, or commit completely to the dream standing right in front of me.

"Where do we go from here?" I ask softly, knowing the answer will define our future.

Emily looks away, uncertainty clouding her delicate features. "I don't know, Ryan. I just don't know." She sighs, her eyes glistening. "But you're always halfway gone, Ryan. I'm here, planted, while you've got one foot out the door. I need someone who's all in."

My throat tightens. She's right. How can I ask her to wait while I chase my dreams? But I can't imagine life without her bright spirit.

I take her hand, meeting her gaze. "Just give me a little more time?" I plead softly.

Around us, the event continues, a blur of light and sound. But in this moment, it's just me and Emily suspended in uncertainty, our future hanging delicately in the balance.

Emily looks down at our clasped hands, conflict playing across her delicate features. The glow of the string lights casts a soft halo around her blonde hair. Even now, she takes my breath away.

"Time won't change who you are, Ryan," she says finally, her voice tinged with sadness. "You'll always have one eye on the horizon, looking for adventure."

I swallow hard. She really does know me, inside and out.

"But that restless spirit is part of why I fell for you," she continues with a wistful half-smile.

My heart leaps. Is there hope after all?

Gently, I brush a strand of hair from her face. "You tether me, Emily. Your love gives me roots I've never had before."

She shakes her head, but doesn't pull away. "Love shouldn't be a cage, either. I don't want to hold you back."

"You don't!" I insist, squeezing her hand. In the distance, laughter peals.

Emily looks toward the sound, then back at me. "So where does that leave us?"

I take a deep breath. "I don't have all the answers. But I know my heart belongs to you. We'll figure the rest out together."

For a long moment, we stand in silence. Then Emily steps closer, resting her head on my shoulder. My arms encircle her slight frame.

We sway gently to the faint music as the stars bear witness. The future is uncertain, but right now, we have each other.

Chapter 16

Emily

The evening sun casts long shadows across my garden as I kneel among the rose bushes, pruning shears in hand. The fading light makes the pink and red blooms glow, soft petals fluttering in the breeze. This garden is my sanctuary, each flower a reflection of my own heart - beautiful yet fragile.

Tending to the roses, I can't help but think of my past loves. So many promising buds that never fully bloomed, left to wilt on the vine. My heart has weathered harsh seasons, and I've grown wary of offering it sunlight and water again. But keeping it walled off in the dark only leaves me feeling cold and alone.

With a sigh, I clip off a dead flower, tossing it aside. I long for warmth, but the risk of frost terrifies me.

"Evenin' Em!" a familiar voice calls. I glance up to see Sarah ambling down the stone path, her straw sunhat askew. "Brought you some lemonade, thought you could use a break."

"Bless you, honey," I say, taking the cold glass. We settle on the bench under the arbor, surrounded by the heavy aroma of gardenia and honeysuckle.

After a few sips, I set down my drink. "Sarah, can I tell you something?"

She nods, her green eyes gentle.

"I'm scared of getting hurt again. By Ryan. My heart's still tender from the past."

Sarah clasps my hand. "Oh Em, what if this time's different? Sure, you might get stung, but the reward could be so sweet. You gotta take that chance."

I blink back tears. "I'm just so scared of opening up and then losing everything."

"But if you don't open up, you may lose him anyway," Sarah says softly. "Love's always a risk. But a life without it is the greatest loss of all."

I know she's right. I've been hiding away too long. It's time to let my heart bloom again.

Ryan

I step into the quiet sanctuary of the library, inhaling the familiar scent of worn pages and leather bindings. Lily is perched on a stool, sorting through a pile of donations.

"Afternoon, Lily," I say.

She glances up, peering at me over her cat-eye glasses. "Well hey there, Ryan. What brings you in today?"

I lean against the circulation desk. "I was hoping to get your advice on something, if you have a minute."

"For you, always," she says, setting down a dusty encyclopedia. "What's on your mind? That job offer on your mind?"

I explain my dilemma and how it's just gotten worse since I last filled her in - the job offer in the city which I need to give an answer on soon, my growing feelings for Emily. Lily listens intently, her wise gaze never leaving mine.

"I've always thought success meant moving up, no matter what," I say. "But now..."

Lily touches my arm. "The best paths aren't always the ones we plan. You can find happiness in unexpected places - and people. Believe me," she says, gesturing around the library, "I had a dream of joining the circus and having a giant family. It took me a long time to realize my place was here in Sweetwater, and these books are my babies."

I ponder her words. She's right. My priorities are shifting. Success has very quickly come to mean something entirely different.

I pace the worn library carpets, gnawing my lip. "Lily, I'm so torn. The job in the city would be amazing, everything I'd ever dreamed of. But now, there's Emily..."

Lily sets down her book cart, folding her hands. "And you care for her."

"Well yeah but - my career was always number one. I can't throw away everything I've worked for, can I?"

Lily smiles gently. "Ryan, life's about more than shiny job titles and fancy equipment. It's about love, community, fulfillment - things money can't buy. You need to look inside yourself. What really matters most?"

I shove my hands in my pockets. She's right. Success doesn't just mean status and wealth. It means finding joy - maybe here in this small town, with a certain strawberry-blonde nurse.

I meet Lily's knowing gaze. "Yeah. I think I know what I need to do."

Lily gives my arm a supportive squeeze before I head out the door.

I walk slowly along the moonlit shore of Clearwater Lake, seeking solitude to think. This quiet spot is where I first started falling for Emily, during our stargazing date months ago. I settle on the worn wooden dock, gazing out at the still black water. It mirrors my pensive mood.

I think of my family's expectations - go to the best schools, become a renowned surgeon. I think of my own ambitions - prestige, wealth, status.

But then I think of Emily. Her warm smile, her selfless spirit, our easy rapport. I never expected to find that here, in this sleepy town. She makes me happier than any fancy job title could.

My priorities are shifting. What matters most now - a loving partner, a sense of home and community? Or cold ambition? Emily, or the distant approval of family?

The choice terrifies me. But my heart knows.

I sit alone as the peaceful night envelops me. The hushed lake calms my swirling thoughts.

But inside, I'm torn. Weighing old dreams of success against new-found joy.

"What do I really want?" I whisper.

Love? Or the career I've spent years chasing? This promotion could change everything. But Emily already has.

Could love be worth altering my life's path? Is it more important than status?

The stillness holds no answers. Only the quiet lapping of water. I breathe deep, listening to my conflicted heart. Choosing won't be easy. But I know what matters most now.

Chapter 17

Emily

The morning sun filters through the canopy of oak trees that line Main Street, dappling the sidewalk with patches of light as I make my way into town. I know this route by heart - past Edna's Quilt Shop, the hardware store, the diner where Ryan and I shared our first milkshake. Each familiar storefront stirs up memories as poignant as the magnolias blooming in the square.

I wave to Old Jack whittling on his porch swing and to Clara arranging pies in the bakery window. My footsteps feel heavy, weighted with hesitation, but I push onward. It's now or never. I can't let fear block my path to happiness any longer.

"Mornin' Emily!" Betty Sue chirps from her perch outside the post office. "You headed over to see that handsome fella of yours?"

"Yes ma'am, I surely am," I say with a nervous laugh.

"Well, you give him my best, ya hear? Don't let that one get away!"

"I'll do my best, Betty Sue," I assure her, quickening my pace. My heart flutters inside my chest like a caged songbird. I'm not letting fear cage me anymore.

The park comes into view, its old oaks swaying gently in the breeze. And there on our favorite bench is Ryan, looking as fine as ever. It's now or never...

Ryan

I settle onto the weathered bench, its wood smoothed by seasons gone by. Around me, the town park breathes with the easy rhythm of a summer morning. Leaves rustle in the breeze as a redbird's trill floats by. It's a pocket of tranquility amidst my recent storms.

I've always found the outdoors to be the best place to sort through my thoughts, ever since I was a boy tossing stones into the duck pond. Now I sift through memories of Emily - her honey-laden laugh, the way sunlight catches in her hair. I recall our stroll around the harvest fair, cider and kettle corn in hand, in step to the fiddler's reel, Emily's eyes sparkling as she coaxed me into a dance.

How could I be so foolish, being so focused on my career that I'm risking letting her slip away? Chasing flashy dreams that will no doubt leave me empty, when all I long for is right here.

I think of Grandad's old saying, "Don't go searching for diamonds when you've already got gold." Emily is my gold. My heart knows now what it's always known - she's my light, my home. I want to build a life with her in this little town that raised her. No more running. My roots are transplanted here. She's here.

The certainty settles into my bones. I've been chasing the wrong dream - but I'm awake now. Maybe it's not too late to make things right. I have to try.

Emily

I spot Ryan sitting alone on the wooden bench by the duck pond, looking contemplative. This spot under the sprawling oak holds so many memories for us. As I approach, butterflies swirl in my stomach. It's now or never.

I clear my throat softly. "Hey stranger."

Ryan looks up, surprise flashing across his face. "Emily! I was just ...thinking about you."

I settle next to him on the bench, leaves skittering across the ground in the breeze. "I've been thinking about you, too."

We're both quiet for a moment, the murmur of the pond filling the space between us. I take a steadying breath.

"Ryan, I know I was harsh the other day. It came from a place of hurt. But the truth is...I miss you. I miss us."

Ryan turns to me, his hazel eyes searching mine. "Me too, Em. More than you know. I think I lost my way for a bit. But you...you're my compass."

I feel a swell of emotion. "I was scared. Scared of losing what we have if things changed. But I realized - I don't want to lose this. I don't want to lose you."

Ryan takes my hand, calloused and warm. "You won't. You're my heart, Emily. If you'll still have me, I want to make this work. I'm willing to take that leap if you are."

I smile through tears. "I am. I'm still scared but - I want to try. I want to build something real together, here in Sweetwater. I know I've been here way longer, but it's where we both belong now."

Ryan pulls me into an embrace. For the first time in weeks, I feel whole.

"Then let's do it," he whispers.

We sit entwined on our bench, leaves dancing, hope reborn. The future is uncertain but we'll face it together.

Chapter 18

Ryan

The fluorescent lights flickered on as I enter the quiet clinic, the empty waiting room greeting me like an old friend. Running my hand along the faded upholstery, I feel a swell of affection for this place that has become my home over the past year. The early morning sun filters through the blinds, bathing everything in a warm, hopeful glow. Today is a new beginning.

With a deep breath, I settle into my office chair and pick up the phone, dialing the too-familiar number of the hospital in the city that's offered me the job. My heart pounds as it rings.

"Good afternoon, this is Marie speaking, how may I direct your call?" chirps the receptionist.

"Hello Marie, it's Dr. Ryan Mitchell calling for Dr. Klein. I'm returning his call from last week about the position." My voice sounds steady, belying the nerves twisting my gut.

"One moment, I'll transfer you now."

I exhale slowly, picturing Dr. Klein's smug face in my mind's eye. We never saw eye to eye, even during my residency where I worked alongside him. But I know he respects my approach to medicine, and there's no doubt in his mind that I'm going to accept his offer.

"Dr. Mitchell, so glad you called back," his nasal voice fills my ear. "Have you given any more thought to our offer? I know it's a big move, but I really think you'll thrive here."

I smile ruefully, knowing what needs to be said. "I appreciate the offer Dr. Klein, but I won't be taking the job. My place is here."

"Here? In that tiny clinic?" He sounds incredulous. "But think of the opportunities here! The salary, the prestige, the-"

"I've made my decision. This town needs me, and I need it too. More than I realized. Thank you again for thinking of me, but my home is here now."

I can picture him sputtering on the other end of the line, but I simply say goodbye and hung up. Leaning back in my chair, I feel a wave of peace wash over me. I'm finally home.

I take a deep breath as I walk up the stone pathway to Emily's light blue Victorian house, admiring the lush gardens surrounding it. Hydrangeas and roses bloom in a riot of color, and the scent of jasmine hangs sweetly in the air. This garden is Emily's pride and joy, a reflection of her nurturing spirit.

I find her on her knees in the soil, wisps of hair escaping her braid as she tends to the plants.

"Well hey there," she smiled up at me, her face smudged with dirt. "To what do I owe the pleasure?"

I crouch down beside her. "I have some news. Big news."

She raises her eyebrows, sitting back on her heels. I can feel that she's nervous about what I'm about to say.

I take her dirt-smudged hand in mine. "I turned down the job offer. I'm staying here for good."

Her mouth drops open. "But what about the advanced medicine? That was your dream job!"

"It was," I admit. "But dreams change. This town, these people..." I squeeze her hand gently. "You. You're my dream now."

Tears spring to her eyes even as she gives a delighted laugh. "Oh, Ryan!"

She throws her arms around me, and I hold her close, breathing in the scent of jasmine and Emily. I've found my home, here with her.

Emily pulled back, looking up at me with those enormous hazel-flecked eyes of hers.

"I can't believe it," she says, her voice hushed. "You're really staying?"

I brush a smudge of dirt from her cheek. "I'm really staying. For you, for this town - it just feels right."

She blinks back happy tears, then laughs. "Well, we'd better start planning then!"

Taking my hand, she leads me over to the porch swing. As we settle in, a sense of peace washes over me. I'm home.

"I was thinking we could expand the clinic," I say. "Add another doctor, see more patients. Really make it the heart of healthcare for Sweetwater and its neighboring towns."

Emily nods, enthusiasm lighting up her face. "That's perfect! Folks around here think so highly of you, ever since you first came."

"And you?" I ask. "Any dreams you want to make reality?"

She smiles softly. "With you by my side, I feel like anything's possible."

We sit in cozy silence for a moment, the creak of the swing and the buzz of hummingbirds our soundtrack.

"I love you, Ryan," Emily say suddenly, squeezing my hand. "I know I'm not supposed to say it yet, but I can't hold it in."

My heart swells fit to bursting. "I love you too, Emily. With all that I am."

We come together in a kiss filled with promise, hope blooming brightly like the flowers surrounding us. The future unfurls before us, rich with possibility.

Hand in hand, Emily and I strolled down Main Street, the morning sun warming the sidewalks. She pauses every so often, calling out cheerful hellos to the shopkeepers just opening up for the day.

"Good morning, Clara!" Emily waves at the owner of the bakery, who beams back.

"Well hey there, Dr. Emily! And who's this fine gentleman with you?" Clara asks.

"This is Dr. Ryan. My partner," Emily replies, her eyes shining as she introduces me.

"Wonderful to meet you!" Clara pumps my hand enthusiastically. "Any fellow of Emily's is a friend of mine. Y'all come by later for some apple pie, it's fresh out the oven."

"We'd love to, thanks Clara," I say, warmed by the kindness of this stranger.

We continue on, Emily greeting more people - the pharmacist, the postman, the owner of the hardware store. With each introduction, I feel myself being woven further into the fabric of this little town. I'd met some of them in passing at various town events, but this somehow feels more formal, more meaningful.

At the park, we sit on a bench and watch the local kids play. Emily and I chat about getting to know them as patients.

"Before you know it, they'll be calling you Dr. Ryan too," Emily says.

I smile, picturing those little faces. "I'd like that."

As we walk back, I feel a sense of belonging that I've never known before. With Emily, I'm not just in a town, but a home.

Our hands swing between us, steps perfectly in sync. The future unfurls before us, rich with the promise of togetherness. I'm finally where I belong.

Chapter 19

Emily

The scent of cinnamon and apples fills my nose as I step into the community center. Sarah greets me with a wide grin, her curly hair bouncing as she rushes over.

"Emily! We've been waiting for you, sugar plum. Come see how pretty it's all coming together."

I follow Sarah into the main hall, and my breath catches. Crisp white linens cover the tables, each adorned with mason jars overflowing with wildflowers. Fairy lights twinkle from the rafters, and a handmade banner stretches across the front of the room reading "Congratulations Emily & Ryan!"

"Oh my word, y'all have outdone yourselves," I say, taking it all in. This place that's been so meaningful in my life looks more magical than I could've imagined.

Lily appears carrying a tray of peach cobblers, the sweet aroma making my mouth water. "We wanted everything to be just perfect for you," she says.

Max comes over, giving my shoulder a squeeze. "No one deserves it more than you two."

I feel tears prick my eyes. To have the love and support of this community means everything. Laughter and chatter fills the space as more folks trickle in—familiar faces that have become like family.

Sarah loops her arm through mine. "Just think, very soon you'll be Mrs. Ryan Mitchell!"

I grin from ear to ear. After the long winding road that brought us here, I can hardly believe we've taken the plunge and committed to each other. But as I look around at the people who make this place so special, I know Ryan and I have found where we belong.

Sarah squeezes my arm gently as more people fill the community center, the buzz of excited chatter growing. I spot Billie Mae from the diner, who slips me a wink as she arranges a spread of all my favorite comfort foods on one of the tables.

"Y'all come get yourself a plateful before it's all gone!" she calls out in her honey-sweet voice.

I make my way through the crowd, exchanging warm hugs and laughing at memories shared. This place, these people - they're everything to me.

Max taps his glass loudly to get everyone's attention. "If I could have y'all gather round, I'd like to say a few words about our girl Emily here, and her fella Ryan."

The room falls silent as all eyes turn to Max. He clears his throat, a twinkle in his eye. "Now I've known Miss Emily here for...well, forever it seems." A chuckle ripples through the crowd. "And I can't think of anyone more deserving of finding a love like she's found with Ryan."

I feel a lump form in my throat, tears pooling in my eyes. Max has been like a big brother to me all these years. To have his blessing means the world.

"So let's raise a glass to Emily and Ryan, and wish them all the happiness in the world!" Max concludes, lifting his glass.

"To Emily and Ryan!" everyone cheers in unison, the bond of this community enveloping me in its warmth. This is where I'm meant to be., and

I slip away from the crowd, the sounds of laughter and happy chatter fading behind me as I make my way down the quiet hallway. I just need a moment to myself, to catch my breath and take it all in.

I find an empty Sunday school classroom, sunlight filtering in through the windows. I sink down into one of the tiny chairs, leaning my head back against the wall and closing my eyes.

A few minutes later, I hear the door creak open. I open my eyes to see Ryan's handsome face peering in.

"There you are," he says with that crooked smile I love. "I was wondering where you'd run off to."

He comes over and sits in the chair next to mine, taking my hand in his.

"Needed a break from all the hoopla?" he asks.

I nod, interlacing my fingers with his. "It's just...a lot. In the best way. But overwhelming too."

Ryan strokes his thumb over the back of my hand. "I know what you mean. But it sure is something to feel so loved."

"It really is," I say softly.

We sit in silence for a few moments, the distant hum of the party like a soundtrack.

"You know what I can't stop thinking about?" Ryan says, turning to look deep into my eyes. "How lucky I am. To have found you. To get to spend my life with my best friend."

Tears fill my eyes again and I lift his hand to my lips, kissing it gently.

"Oh Ryan. I'm the lucky one," I reply. "You make me happier than I ever dreamed I could be."

He leans in and kisses me tenderly, a promise of all the bliss yet to come. I know as long as we're together, I'm home.

Chapter 20

Emily

I nestle into Ryan's side, sinking into the soft cushions of our new couch. Our living room is a patchwork quilt of our merged lives - my embroidered pillows alongside his leather recliner, my bookshelves packed with medical texts and his action novels.

"I can't believe this is really our house," I say, letting my head rest on his shoulder.

Ryan smiles, his arm wrapping around me. "Me either, Em. But I'm sure glad it is."

Our eyes meet and my heart flutters like it's our first date all over again. I know Ryan's the one for me - the way he selflessly takes care of his mom after his dad passed, the late nights he spends helping me plan for the expansion of my speech therapy practice, that lopsided grin of his that makes me weak in the knees.

"What're you thinking about over there?" Ryan asks.

"Oh, just daydreaming about our future. Like maybe adding a sunroom out back, with big windows and wicker furniture."

Ryan chuckles. "You and your porches. Alright, sunroom it is."

I poke his side playfully. "Well, what about you? Any big career dreams on the horizon?"

Ryan gets a faraway look in his eye. "You know, I've been thinking about integrating some new approaches to the way we do medicine in Sweetwater. There's some equipment that's not prohibitively expensive. And maybe coming up with a mentorship program to inspire the town's young people to consider a career in medicine."

"I think you'd make an amazing mentor." I squeeze his hand supportively. Influences like him can really make a difference in kids' lives.

We chat more about our dreams - the places we'll travel, the family we'll raise. Curled up together, everything seems possible. This house, this life with Ryan - it's everything I've ever wanted. As long as we have each other, I know we'll build something beautiful here.

"Oh shoot, we better get a move on if we're gonna make it to the fundraiser on time," I say, glancing at the clock.

Ryan groans good-naturedly. "Ugh, community events. You know how I get around people."

"Come on, grumpy gills. It'll be fun! We get to show off our lame couple's costume."

I grab Ryan's hand and practically drag him out the door. We're dressed as surgeons - me in blue scrubs and a stethoscope, Ryan in green scrubs and a face mask. Not exactly high fashion, but it gets a laugh from the crowd.

At the town hall, Ryan and I mingle with our neighbors. He charms little old ladies while I fawn over babies in strollers. I chat with Sarah about her classroom's new pet turtle.

"You two really do make quite the team," Sarah says, smiling.

Ryan slides an arm around my waist. "We do alright," he says, giving me a peck on the cheek.

On the walk home, we pause to admire the sunset over the lake, the sky awash in pink and orange. Ryan slips his hand in mine as we stroll beneath the golden maples lining the street.

After, curled up on the couch with mugs of tea, Ryan asks about my day at the clinic. I tell him about Theo's progress, and he tells me about little Timmy's ear infection and Mrs. Patterson's arthritis flare-up.

When I speak, he listens intently, like he always does. With Ryan, I feel truly heard and understood. As we sit together in the quiet of our home, I'm filled with a profound sense of belonging. This town, this man - they're everything I've been searching for. My long journey has led me here, to contentment.

Ryan

I take a sip of tea, savoring the warmth.

"You know, when I first got to town, I never imagined feeling so at home," I say. "After years of wandering, I wasn't sure I belonged anywhere."

Emily squeezes my hand. "I'm glad you took a chance on this place. On us."

"Me too." I nestle against her shoulder. "I can't picture being anywhere else now."

We chat more about our early days in town - my first weeks at the clinic, settling in. We laugh about fumbling first interactions, false starts, and gradual openings.

"I knew I was a goner that first time you smiled at me," I say.

"Even with files all over the floor?" I tease.

"Especially with files all over the floor."

Later, as we climb into bed, I kiss her tenderly.

"You make me happier than I ever dreamed I could be," I whisper.

"Ditto," she whispers, and my heart swells.

I wraps her in my arms and we drift off, feeling safe, loved, and incredibly grateful for this simple yet beautiful life we're building together.

Emily

I nestle closer to Ryan as we sit curled up on the couch, mugs of tea warming our hands. The golden glow of the lamp casts our living room in cozy light as a gentle rain taps the windows.

"What a beautiful sound," I say softly.

Ryan nods, taking a slow sip of tea. "Rain always reminds me of new beginnings."

I consider his words. This house, this relationship - it does feel like a fresh start for both of us.

"You're right," I reply. "It's cleansing, in a way. Washing away the past."

Ryan sets down his mug and takes my hand. "Emily, you've brought so much joy into my life. I can't imagine taking on the future without you by my side."

My breath catches at the emotion in his voice.

"Oh, Ryan..." I whisper.

"Marry me?" He asks, eyes searching mine.

"Yes!" I exclaim, surging forward to kiss him deeply.

Rain patters, tea goes cold, but we remain wrapped up in each other, the promise of tomorrow glowing brighter than ever.